FALL & WINTER 2024
VOLUME 52 NUMBER 1

Editor
Kathryn Kirkpatrick

Managing Editor
Matthew Wemberley

Assistant Editor
Maddie Ball

Production Assistance
Natalie Foreman

Editorial Board
Joseph Bathanti, Craig Fisher, Lynn Doyle, Sarah Beth Hopton, Alex Pitofsky, Zackary Vernon

Advisory Board
Houston A. Baker, Martin Espada, Jaki Shelton Green, Lee Gutkind, Ed Madden, Heather Ross Miller, Robert Morgan, Simon Ortiz, Nancy Huddleston Packer, R.T. Smith

In fall 2024, *Cold Mountain Review* relaunched in an open access online format hosted by ASU's Belk Library. Print formats of each issue are available through the University of North Carolina Press. For more information, including submission guidelines, please visit https://cold-mountain-review.pubpub.org/.

Cold Mountain Review is published biannually in the Department of English at Appalachian State University. Support from ASU's Office of Academic Affairs and College of Arts and Sciences enables *CMR*'s learning and publications program. The views and opinions expressed in *CMR* do not necessarily reflect those of university trustees, administration, faculty, students, or staff.

Copyright © 2024 by Appalachian State University
ISSN 1547-5972
ISBN 978-1-4696-9161-9 (paperback)

Cold Mountain Review is indexed in the MLA International Bibliography and Humanities international Complete and is a member of The Council of Literary Magazines and Presses. Typefaces used are TBD, designed by TBD. Typeset by TBD. *CMR* logo designed by Sarah McBryde.

CONTENTS

KATHRYN KIRKPATRICK
Editor's Note for Retrospective Issue
Revived and Then Set Free

BASIL KING
Artist's Statement for Perch #12

POETRY

R.T. SMITH
Parkinson's Sparrow

JAMES SILAS ROGERS
Trapped Sparrow, O'Hare Airport

PATRICK HICKS
Umbilical Cord

LORY BEDIKIAN
At My Mother's Dresser

BENITO DEL PLIEGO
Yellowstone: sobre piedra amarilla.

HILDA DOWNER
Picking Cherries up Howell Holler

SALLY ATKINS
In the House of My Great-Grandmother

SARAH KENNEDY
First Child

JANET LEE WARMAN
In Search of Hills

M. SOLEDAD CABALLERO
Remembering

FALL & WINTER 2024

ED MADDEN
  Like a thief

G.C. WALDREP
  Harvest Crew

TODD DAVIS
  Morning Poem

STEVEN R. COPE
  Oshon

LINDA MALNACK
  The Physics of Heaven

R.T. SMITH
  Ruin

CATHERINE YOUNG
  Gathering Acorns, Hoarding Words

ANNE MARIE MACARI
  What Will You Feed Them?

CHRISTIE COLLINS
  Elegy

LIZ ROBBINS
  Shadow Box

CYNTHIA ATKINS
  Elegy for a Scarecrow

RITA QUILLEN
  october dusk

DAID CHILDERS
  American Dusk

VIRGIL SUÁREZ
  Callas

ROBERT MORGAN
  Pockets

COLD MOUNTAIN REVIEW

CATHERINE CARTER
Crow Cosmogony

MARSHA TRUMAN COOPER
Nesting Boxes

JEFF HARDIN
Woodsmoke

R.T. SMITH
Raptor

TIM APPLEGATE
The Owl

REBECCA BAGGETT
Opossums

THOMAS PIRKLE
In the Kitchen

LESLEY WHEELER
Asexual Reproduction

R.T. SMITH
Watauga Augury

ANNIE WOODFORD
In the City Woods

KEVIN KECK
Anniversary of Your Father's Death

PAUL MULDOON
Redknots

ROSE MCLARNEY
You Must Know Things By Their Moving Away

GUSTAVO PÉREZ FIRMAT
Old Octopus

FALL & WINTER 2024

ESSAY

LINDA HOGAN
Black Walnut: Sweet Blood History

R.T. SMITH
Gooseneck Loosestrife

CONTRIBUTORS

KATHRYN KIRKPATRICK

Revived and Then Set Free

With this new issue of *Cold Mountain Review*, we relaunch the journal as a biannual publication. We're proud to now have *CMR* located among Appalachian State's Belk Library open access journals, and we'll also be featuring print-on-demand copies of each issue through UNC Press. How fortunate to have found such a good home with such gifted partners!

With this retrospective issue we take several steps back the better to leap forward or, who knows, maybe to lift off and fly: there are birds everywhere in this gathering of poems and one lyric essay—pigeons, sparrows, crows, bluebirds, owls, redknots, and finches. Our cover image, "Perch #12," comes from a series inspired in part by that most familiar of all urban birds, pigeons, by an artist, Basil King, who studied at one of our region's most famous schools, Black Mountain College. "Perch #12" is housed with the third of our fine university partners, ASU's Turchin Center for the Visual Arts.

Though the other animals are often on our minds at *CMR*, we didn't set out to find them as we sifted through the decades of back issues. Yet like an *I Ching* cast, with each trip through fifty years and more of a journal, work re-emerges to suit the moment. From the hands of two poets, a retrospective issue largely of poetry has emerged, with poems ranging from the 1970s, the first decade of CMR's founding, to today and three new poems by one of the journal's founders, R.T. Smith. Aptly, it's R.T.'s poems old and new, that have given this issue wings. In "Parkinson's Sparrow," the narrator finds the poise we will all someday need in the face of fading health, even as his poem perches between the actual life of a delicate sparrow and the lessons that tiny life brings: "I recall the bird's secret / and see the tremors I know — / disease and its sorrows — / diminished beside a single / sparrow one cold day / revived and then set free."

Providing habitat for the birds, trees also grow from this issue, the pinecones of Benito Del Pliego's fire germinating after fire to produce in "Yellowstone: sobre piedra amarilla" a line like a Gary Snyder-inspired Zen kōan: "Your strength will be born from your / nothingness." Annie Woodford's "In the City Woods" sounds companionate notes between humans and trees – "These trees store a record / of the same floods as us in their rings" – that Linda Hogan's "Black Walnut: A Sweet Blood History" powerfully expands. In Hogan's essay black walnut trees literally hold the earth and myriad lives, human and nonhuman, in place: "Their magnificent underground roots spread out a long distance to hold the moist bottomland soil intact."

Seasons, cycles, births, and elegies are all here. Like the piles of debris that still line our roads in the Blue Ridge Mountains after the water and wind of Hurricane Helene swept through in late September, the natural world won't let us forget our human limits. We'll need the resiliences of community so evident after that storm to weather what's ahead. And in that world poetry will always have a role. As Catherine Young observes in "Gathering Acorns, Hoarding Words," "humankind over millennia has held the world together/ with words, a continuous thread woven through hymns and sagas, / echoed across fjords and geyser fields, *pastures* and yards." Italicizing the words, largely from the natural world, OUP's *Oxford Junior Dictionary* jettisoned from the word hoard of children, Young's poem works to include and restore them.

For over half a century, *Cold Mountain Review* has provided a home for writing that explores the interplay of the social and ecological, of what it means to live inside a human skin alongside so many others, human and nonhuman alike. We keep staying with the trouble, building and rebuilding with nature's resilience. We want to last the duration.

December 8, 2024

BASIL KING

Artist's Statement for Perch #12

"Perch #12" is in a series of birds I have been painting and drawing since the 1960s. I don't paint or draw one particular bird. I paint birds, their shapes. Pigeons have been important to me since I was a boy. They fascinate me. Their timing, the way they handle crowds on city streets always amazes me. They manage to get out of our way at the last moment.

November 27, 2024

FALL & WINTER 2024

R.T. SMITH

Parkinson's Sparrow

I call this trembling
arrowing my arm
"Parkinson's Sparrow"
after a bird that flew
into my window
last winter, against her
own reflection, shattering
my reverie on the snow.
In my cupped palms
she was stillness and heat.
Shaking, I began to blow,
the only remedy I knew,
my breath across her brow
and breast a warm
soundless speech,
until wet wings stirred,
then fluttered in a fury
against my fingers.
I opened up slowly
to see the rust-brown
feathers, precise beak
an emphatic black eye.
Gone in a heartbeat, she
headed for the holly hedge
uttering her flight cry —
seet, seet, seet. She printed
on my skin a memory
akin to these tremors
keeping me from sleep,
making my hands
and tenor voice unsteady.
"Resigned now," I tell
my friends and family,
but ever reeling on the edge
of dread and self-pity, until
I recall the bird's secret
and see the tremors I know —
disease and its sorrows —
diminished beside a single

sparrow one cold day
revived then set free.
Lord have mercy.
Lord have mercy on me.

JAMES SILAS ROGERS

Trapped Sparrow, O'Hare Airport

Bede or some such saint said that all
this earthly life amounts to is a bird
flying in and out the windows of a hall.
That's an arresting thought, this morning
on the ground in this non-place where
the highest good is to be on time
and no one asks what time itself is good for.
Today, Bede might have preferred
to use the metaphor of changing planes;
we hurry around while being transferred
from one gate to another, then sit –
a pinball waiting to be batted out
of our stasis and onto the scheduled
crest of a tide. On the other hand, the system
works, most of the time. This morning
is one of those frozen-in spaces, owing
to a mechanical delay. A ten-year-old boy
across from me is immersed in a handheld
game. I wonder if he knows the difference
between his toy reality and the flight
for which we both wait. Do I?
Idling at the gate, the book I am reading
involves medieval wonder tales
of talking birds. They were easy to believe,
nine hundred years ago. An eagle
would climb onto a sinning king's
dinner table and give him a fierce
but pious scolding. Or a white dove
would give comfort at an empty cradle.
Once, talking crows were common,
miracles that caught no one off guard,
just ordinary stories that got told
in grocery stores and pubs. I close my book
and as I do, a small, feathered blur,
a house sparrow, flies overhead, streaking
straight down the mezzanine.
Were I more optimistic, I'd think
the bird could find a way out

of its airport stir, but I have my doubts.
Morning sunlight pours through vast
windows, but the bird, like the rest of us
is caught on the inside of the glass –
no weather, no breeze. I imagine a serf
in the age of Alfred, and how he might
look up from the surrounding mud
to see a passing lark, and be reminded
by its song and its disappearance into
the distance that, yes, escape
was still possible somewhere in the world.
On Concourse C, I am far from certain
there is any place the sparrow could go;
but it leaves a whisper in its wake.

Vol. 44, no. 1, 2015

PATRICK HICKS

Umbilical Cord

for my adopted son from South Korea

When you arrived from South Korea,
the adoption agency sent over your umbilical cord.
This purple stump, shriveled like a raisin,
is clasped in a plastic vise –
its jawed teeth biting down on that moment
when you were snipped away
from your birth mother.

For almost a year it has followed you from
hospital to orphanage to foster home,
then across the wide Pacific to our little house.
It nuzzles in the attic now, waiting,
waiting, I suppose, until you find it as a man
and study its wrinkled shape. This dried root
binds you to a moment of loss, it is the gap
between your two different worlds.

Volume 40, no. 2, 2012

LORY BEDIKIAN

At My Mother's Dresser

I lift my five-year-old
body on the chair to watch
her fingers lift blush powder,

(burnt rose), to her face.
The strokes seem counted
out, maybe twenty brushes

on each cheekbone. In the mirror
I mimic her, but she doesn't
smile, and instead, dabs

perfume on her wrists and neck,
combs back her stiff, chestnut
hair cut short above the ear,

a bird's nest, a crown, adjusts
an opalescent button in the silk
blouse's eye, the stockings

already torn. Without a word,
sigh, in haste she chooses
large, red, faux bijou beads

to hide the pale olive in her skin.
I know these things make her
stand apart from the others,

PTA mothers, grocery clerks,
the women in afternoon dramas.
I will grow to resemble her: our eyebrows

too dark, two brush strokes of rain
clouds, our noses edged pyramids,
always causing a double look, a glance.

She rubs cream under the eyes'
half-moons, taupe for the lids.
To match her nails (another burnt hue

of red) she fumbles for the final touch
on her mouth. She needs to hurry
before they arrive: the relatives

who have been missing for years,
names mentioned, tossed photos
in a shoebox, phone calls cut short,

people she hated to leave behind
in Syria while she and my father
made the trek to the States.

I know there is something
even more unique about her
than the others, because as she swirls

the lipstick toward her mouth, one
hand smoothes the color on, while
the other dabs the crying that's

begun. She does this without a change
of face, she does this as if it's part
of dressing, of carrying on.

Volume 38, no. 1, 2009

BENITO DEL PLIEGO

Yellowstone: sobre piedra amarilla.

1.
Solo si el abeto arde, la semilla que ascendió
fructifica. El abeto goza de su destrucción y
cree en su cadáver.

No lo quieres saber, pero tus dedos lo
escribieron en el aire infestado de mosquitos:
"Tu vigor nace de tu nada".

2.
Búfalo: piedra de las praderas que respire como
el geiser; en su lomo pasta el prado, se aparean
en él los rios y pelea monte contra monte. Su
testuz soporta el mundo: ni miente ni piensa, es
mucho más cuanto más rumia.

En su hostilidad honesta abre un ojo el musgo y
la roca contempla su propio precipicio.

Búfalo, poeta; búfalo, dador de vida.

3.
La humanidad es un indio surgido do un coágulo de
búfalo. Esta será su nota de despedida: "Te lo
advertí, Cowboy: nadie pastorea sus rebaño hacia
el frío".

BENITO DEL PLIEGO

Yellowstone: on a yellow rock.

1.
Only if the fir burns, its highest seed will blossom. Firs enjoy their death and feed from their own carcasses.

You don't want to acknowledge it, but it was written with your fingers on mosquito-infested air: "Your strength will be born from your nothingness".

2.
Buffalo, prairie stone breathing as a geyser; on his back the fields are put to pasture, on him the rivers mate, and a mountain fights a mountain; On his head the world is resting. He doesn't lie, he doesn't doubt, he is more as he chews.

Upon his hostile honesty, the moss opens its eye, and the rock contemplates its own falling.

Buffalo, poet; Buffalo, life-giver.

3.
Humanity is an Indian boy born from a buffalo. This will be his good-bye note: "I told you, Cowboy: no one should take his herds towards the winter".

Volume 36, no. 2, 2008

HILDA DOWNER

Picking Cherries up Howell Holler

Unlike the hybrids darkly maroon in stores,
these that glowed red from the inside
followed a delicate translucent white.
The Juliana brooch my grandmother wore–
roan rhinestones of the cherry tree
donned her old home place.
Rudolph noses, their guidance
balanced the branch's shaky tight wires
as we reached toward more light.

My tongue felt for the seam of the pit
long after the last rags of fruit weathered.
Bare feet felt for sandy ruffles in the road.
Darkness smelled where a spring
poked its finger through the bank.
Then, I spit out all possibility
from deep in the mountains,
deep within me,
deeper still in childhood,
the meager attempt
to give something more
than was given to me.

Volume 36, no. 2, 2008

SALLY ATKINS

In the House of My Great-Grandmother

Broken stones and brick from the great twin chimneys,
All that remain of the house. The land still slopes gently
All the way to the river. I remember how large it looked
To me as a child, that old farmhouse almost as tall
As the giant sycamore tree, stark and bare
Like the mountain women
Who cooked and sewed and bore children in it.

I remember three porches, three sides of life:
The back porch for kitchen work, the side
For tying up horses, feeding hired hands,
The front porch where family sat in the evenings
On feather feed sack pillows in rocking chairs
While neighbors visited and great uncle Braxton
Played the banjo.

In my dream I am cleaning this house,
Letting in air and sunshine,
Cooking cornbread in the old wood stove.
I am making a place for myself.
I am thinking that here
In the presence of the grandmothers
Is where I want to live.

Volume 31, no. 1, 2002

SARAH KENNEDY

First Child

The night you are born I lie awake
    while you curl, dozing, in my arm.
        Your father's gone home to his cabin

in the woods, but I'm content here. The nurses,
    murmuring about some other woman, sound
        like my sisters, laughing among themselves.

Stretching, open-mouthed, you turn,
    and I almost call out. Barely eighteen,
        with a husband twice my age who believes

motherhood will settle my mind—what
    do I know about babies? A streetlamp
        hits the pink bow someone has knotted

in your hair and I think *I'm tied to him*
    forever now. A siren from downtown
        rouses me to the window where I study

the city I roamed before my dad decided
    he needed to own a farm. You bite down
        on my nipple, hungry for more. My eyes burn

and my stitches itch, but I don't pull back.
    Cabbies still honk right after the traffic lights
        change. My city-girl angles have melted to belly

and breast. I unwrap you, fold by fold,
    testing your bones' hardness, though the doctor
        has said I need sleep, my blood busy churning to milk.

(*from Flow Blue, Elixir Press, 2002*)

Volume 30, no. 2, 2002

JANET LEE WARMAN

In Search of Hills

Those nights on the plains I would drive
for hours in search of hills.
One gentle rise was all I asked
to rock me
one rippled edge
one slope.
My gaze would wander out
always level, unflinchingly level;
and when I felt that hours or miles had disappointed enough
I'd turn a grudging U,
my tires throwing dirt onto the edge of some farmer's field,
say a prayer, cast hope over my shoulder
up to some imaginary height,
then plummet down through blue to dust again.

Volume 24, no. 1, 1995

M. SOLEDAD CABALLERO

Remembering

      I
I remember it was you
who read aloud to me
and taught me how to see and
feel the words.
And you who sang to me
in your subtle, aching voice
about the lonely queen
and her three soft daughters.
And it was you
who showed me how
to believe in quiet fairies and
talking stars and
even Santa Claus.
I even learned to smile
from you.
I learned that brittle, lonely smile
from you.

      II
And I remember you,
you smiled through everything–
the tears and anger and
the miles
of nothing
but dry, Oklahoma prairie grass.
You smiled
through leaving
the soil that
you for three decades
called home.
You smiled
through leaving
your life behind
in the greyness
of the Andes.
But I remember
the sighs too and
the way

you used to whisper
mi pais querido
into the night air.
I remember Mother
I remember.

ED MADDEN

Like a thief

i
The barn behind the house has fallen in,
honeysuckle and rambling rose crawling

across the ruins. What surprises more,
though, is the way that things have grown—

the pines planted along the yard's edge
when he was a child are huge now, festooned

with cones; the honey locust, scrawny redbud
grown beyond the spindly things in memory.

ii
He knows that thieves have broken in the house
on a morning just like this, a morning when

they knew it would be empty. They stole the guns,
jewelry, money—what they could find, left

the door open. A morning full of hymns,
the day of the Lord. Like a thief, he thinks.

iii
The rental car idles in the drive.
She sees the man beside him in the car.

She knows who he is, and what.
She stays behind the window, in the dark.

iv
A strange calm hovers above the yard,
June's noon a dim shimmer of heat

and humming bugs, a tense stillness ready
to disintegrate, crumble into regrets.

He doesn't try the door, wonders if
his key would fit, if the locks were changed.

v
A basket big enough to hold a child,
white pine latticed beneath a lid,

a basket full of nothing—the air, the heat,
perhaps a card, apologies. Something

to abandon. He found it in an antique
shop, littered with small and broken things.

vi
Surprised by the way that things have grown.
The rental car idles in the drive.

vii
He leaves the basket at the back door—
a basket big enough to hold a child—

a gift for his mother. He doesn't know
his father went to church alone, he doesn't

know she's there, doesn't see her looking
from the kitchen window as he drives away.

Volume 30, no. 1, 2001

G.C. WALDREP

Harvest Crew

Nights, we don't talk much.
Those with beds take
some measure of sleep, their hands
hardening in the cold dark air,

ears stopped against
the wind's consistent negations
except for those moments
in the ordinal hours

when some bird, alarmed
by nightmare or predation,
comes to knowledge of itself
beyond the scope of its small

and fine-boned imagination,
sending out its call brief
but recognizable, sudden,
aloft, across the fields–

we wait for that,
hope's music or something
like it, what trains the ear
to hear in day.

Volume 26, no. 2, 1998

TODD DAVIS

Morning Poem

Blackberries still hang in the darkest
creases of the trellis, each dimple swelled
to bursting. The black-eyed Susans are mostly
black, their petals' yellow tresses already rotted.
Goldfinches wander the air, meditate
upon the cone flower's sharp seed, trying
to discern if it's time to leave. This early,
before anyone has opened their doors, I watch
birds sidle up to sunflowers, even cosmos,
while cricket-song comes through the screens
like fog in the belly of this valley. I've been
making jam most of the last month, and the jars
from last night's batch have been talking, lids
sinking toward sweetness with a satisfied
metallic song. The weatherman warns of frost,
so after the air warms this morning, I'll scoop
the last bits of black from the vine's green string,
press the potato-masher, syrup from these berries
rendered into a bowl the color of nightshade.
Other birds will dawdle through, but none
will be dressed as brightly as the finches
who helped greet the dawn. If there's any
consolation in the dying we must do, then let it be
stored on a shelf in a raised glass jar, adorned
with pictures of strawberries and cherries,
grapes and pears, the pale seeds that fix
in the cracks of our teeth, floating in a sticky
infusion we lick from the ends
of our breakfast spoons.

Volume 37, no. 2, 2009

STEVEN R. COPE

Oshon

Now I am brought to this edge
and have felt the unknown hand
grip the underside of my belly.
I have risen impaled,
unearthly posed,
thrust toward a kingdom.

I have flown grasshopper wings
cross-ways in the sun
and have believed I was a bird.
I have stretched amazingly;
done enormous feats of the soul.
But it is too much, too little. . . .

Now I am brought to this edge
and have heard you howling from the water.
I have left the water running.
I have crawled to you on my knees.
I have licked your hand, waiting.
I am of whose kingdom, whose kingdom?

Volume 14, no. 1, 1986

LINDA MALNACK

The Physics of Heaven

If the scent of fig and hyacinth and fallen olive
leaves stays pinned
to earth, yet we, once crushed, ascend–
creatures, with conscience, ready to believe

and rise–we may find in our spirited climb
brushed by angels' wings,
chafed by the rougher deeds
of our lives, that we too are pungent perfume

distilled by light, drawn into the olfactory
of God; together
we are bowls of withered
leaves and petals, bits of bark, a potpourri:

the universe breathes us in like attar
and breathes us out again as stars.

Volume 27, no. 2, 1999

R.T. SMITH

Ruin

A derelict cottage on the marsh
amid red grass and sandspurs,
swamp haw and lilies.
You can get there by jonboat
or a disused road through the cedars,
and you might survey the dunes
 or study the broken-backed barn,
watch dwarf deer at the salt lick
or search for antiques
in debris. Maybe you'd see
on the beach a farm dog gnawing
a stag's shed antler. Parasites
waste the lemon tree,
its bark and pallid leaves,
and the smallest events of light
across the sound's
wind-distressed waters
invoke the minor episodes
of one remote and simple life. Inside,
the ceiling damp with honey
sags, and you wonder when cracked plaster
will give way and the hive
spill drones onto the kitchen floor.
From the window you can see
if the moon comes up, once more
thin gray over the waves. You can sift
through the midden, imagine
a life reduced to relics—
potsherds, grave toys, stones.

Volume 15, no. 1, 1987

CATHERINE YOUNG

Gathering Acorns, Hoarding Words

> "... there had been a culling of words concerning nature. Under pressure, Oxford University Press revealed a list of the entries it no longer felt to be relevant to a modern-day childhood. The deletions included *acorn, adder, ash, beech, bluebell, buttercup, catkin, conker, cowslip, cygnet, dandelion, fern, hazel, heather, heron, ivy, kingfisher, lark, mistletoe, nectar, newt, otter, pasture and willow.*"
>
> —from Robert McFarlane's "The Word Hoard" in *Landmarks*

I
If children do not know willow,
how will they know the scent
of spearmint, or peppermint in cold spring streams,
or how water flow is shaped
by willow root? And if
they do not hear the word catkin,
how will they hear the bees
as they forage for nectar in willow flowers,
in hazel shrubs, birch trees. If children
do not know acorn,
how will they play in fall
with the scaly cupule of nut on a finger for a hat,
or plant oak trees
that will outlive them?
And *dandelion* – when will they learn
the yellow of a *Helianthus* mirror of sun
or May crowns, or magnificently silken
parachutes –
How might each successive generation
take life lessons to follow wind
and dreams; find open spaces
in which to land and grow?

II
Fern in wood;
heron, lark, kingfisher, in river, sky, sea;
otter in stream and ocean; *cygnet* in reeds,
and all that dwell beside and among us:
humankind over millennia has held the world together
with words, a continuous thread woven through hymns and sagas,
echoed across fjords and geyser fields, *pastures* and yards.

Let us, for all the children, chant your names,
call to your being –
We hold you remembered,
recognized,
real.

ANNE MARIE MACARI

What Will You Feed Them?

Scraping corn till its milk covers
my hands. Silky pile of husks. Tomato,
rosemary, chives from the garden.
Dreaming back far into the flesh of the plant.

How we are plants grown awkward and strange.

We saw the tail hanging from the hawk's
beak as it flew off, an apple protruding
from the mouth of the deer.

I whisked and pounded, sifted
and sliced. It was mortar
for their bones. It was what
we found in the woods.
The egg that fit so well in my palm
and what came out of it.

Fire. Blood. Fungus.
Muscle. Marrow. Greens.
Nuts and garlic, wild carrot.
It's the food inside the food,
the invisible heart of the berry,
how it goes on beating
in the hallways of the body.

When the Complete comes to find me
the one question will be, *What did
you feed them?* As if I could
remember the colors arranged

just so, the balance, a lifetime
of salt thrown into the pot
and whirling there. As if each
bite was language broken
down in the mouth, each word

tasting of its sour its bitter
its sweet, to stem the craving.
What we swallowed all those years—

platter of distress, bowl
of hope. What I chewed—my own
fingers and lip. *What did you feed them?*
I fed them love. *What did you feed them?*
Love and bones, gristle,
sermons, air, mercy,

rain, ice, terror and soup, anger and dandelion
and love. *What did*

you feed them? Go to sleep
in the straw and when you wake up
I will give you something warm in a cup,

I will mix it myself, and when the Complete
finally comes for me I'll have water
hot on the stove, the tea

just right, I'll say I've sucked
the bread of this life
but I'm never full, I'll go
with my mouth open—

(Copyright 2005)
Volume 35, no. 1, 2006

CHRISTIE COLLINS

Elegy

Out of the blue woods
a kitten wandered our way.
Hours later, she died.
We placed her small body
in a pencil box.
We said goodbye, and we meant it.
We covered her with earth and leaves,
orange and yellow, and moved on
until spring brought us back to the same spot.
There, while digging a place to plant a post,
my father unearthed the forgotten grave.
I stooped to the ground amid the browning
underbrush and lifted the cardboard box,
opening the lid before anyone could warn against it.
What should have been nature at play,
dissolving flesh and fur into shapeless matter
was instead nothing but dust and discoloration.
No bones or body.
It was as if the animal had simply chosen
another fate, rising, rounding her back
in a deep stretch before chasing a lightning bug
or horsefly to the next farm.
I've come to think of you in this way:
that maybe just after we left you to rest
on the saddest summer afternoon,
you awoke and decided to instead visit distant
relatives, first in Ipswich and then Nepal,
finding reason after reason
to never come back home.
Maybe just as I say this,
you are walking toward this poem.

LIZ ROBBINS

Shadow Box

We fly north in snow to bury your father. Tall windows of the country house, the lake a hard fogged mirror. I understand parts when you speak. Alone we process negatives: bed pan, stale air, mouth ajar. New the dark irreversibles. Flash of dandelion heads in grass, plastic chairs in shallows. Early summer light close, Dutch-Mastered. But this the usual ragged circle. No blood sacrifice. No tongue or hands cut free to keep secrets. Even the snow not unwhite. But some of us need rage. Talk turns to god, governance, money. The many scales. Near, the fish slowed beneath the ice. Hard to expose. I run the lake, exhaling him, cold twinge above hips. Winter more near. The trees unmoved, I love you. To the new black dress, I'll pin a gold leaf.

Volume 40, no. 1, 2011

CYNTHIA ATKINS

Elegy for a Scarecrow

October's henchman has bled again.
Evenly the straw is strewn
without retribution or shame.

An amplitude of human contact
stitched into the farmer's flannel shirt,
that still smells of apple cores, smoke and hay.

This hired hand without pay, here to usher
in bounty and harvest, where yearning is heard
intermittent as an owl in the barn.

At first frost, face down, he knew his place
and his art, presiding over compost and rue –
the last of the soup stirred in

a lonely widow's kitchen. Last spring
the ghosts of her grown children
sprinkled the seeds in all the wrong places –

but a garden grew just the same.
A snow of willows. The landscape shivers.
He never said a word, but she looked for

his company, understanding his serious business
with the weather – befriending pumpkins
in midnight sun. The crows are inconsolable,

their wings leave stains across the moon.

Volume 38, no. 2, 2010

RITA QUILLEN

october dusk

    the evening dark
    falls all around me
    its warm breath
    casts a shadow on my face

    sitting on my front steps
    I am a candle flame
    drawing moths and mosquitoes
    holding the moments in my cupped hands

    he sits quietly by me
    memories of the day's work
    swift moving color shared
    like fall leaves in the yard

    the potatoes from the garden
    lie scattered in the grass
    tomorrow we will sort them
    and store them for winter

    his hand rests on my neck
    as he slowly stands
    he offers the other dirty hand
    to help me up

    our eyes meet in the fading light
    we go inside
    surrendering to night
    the smell of earth still strong

    Volume 10, no. 1, 1982

DAVID CHILDERS

American Dusk

    On a street in America
    as in Rome, a woman
    whose husband is in Germany
    leaves home.

    The butcher folds his bloody towel
    and sings.
    The banker thinks of sail boats
    on white water.

    Goodnight says the plumber's daughter.
    I love you says the sky.

    Shirtless men under cold front clouds
    watch an orange star
    rise.

    Volume 1, no. 1, 1974

VIRGIL SUÁREZ

Callas

the blue house in Coyoacan, house of blue light, in the bright sun the blue is the kiss of sky, like the birds she so loved which fed from the feeders, sweet nectar attracted the red-throated hummingbirds, her little *angelitos*, and the scent of *taquitos de flor de calabaza* rising from the kitchen on those days she lay in bed and dreamt of her monkey, how it brought him fruit, *jicama* and *chili piquin,* the way he liked it, and she sketched, and read the *retablos* she got from the church, little prayers and get-well wishes, and the pigeons flew up on the sill to coo their songs, a lullaby to ease her into her afternoon nap, and the heat brought her the kind of dog exhaustion she hated, and then the breeze, and a new bouquet of Calla Lilies arrived and the servants brought them to her room, these gauze-like flowers of surrender, of his love, but she knew better; sometimes she held one flower in her hands, took the knife by her night stand and cut a stalk, a slight flick of the wrist and the blood flowed from the stems, and into her own veins, filling her with the sweet pollen of possibility, this magic dust of tenderness, a love so raw it made her tear at the flesh around her chest, exposing the pomegranate fruit, the one he bit each night when they were lovers, a *murcielago* whose hunger pleased her, and she felt whole in the silken blue light, house of longing and surrender.

Volume 28, no. 1, 1999

ROBERT MORGAN

Pockets

I wonder what men did before
their pants had pockets. Where did Keats
for instance put his ink stained hand
to rest its cramp? The priests had sleeves
on their long robes in which to clasp
their mitts in piety. But where
did other men hide sweaty palms
and awkward knuckles standing in
a crowd or sauntering alone
into a strange room? Pockets are
a comfort, not only a place
to hide our nervous itchy fingers
but a refuge of warmth and dark
as cozy as a kitten, always
at sides like holsters for our most
deadly and versatile thumbs. Hands
in pockets are a sign of shyness
and even peacefulness. Hands need
a place of privacy and safety,
a place of repose and muffling, need
dens in which to burrow deep
with coins and keys and pocket knives
and puffs of lint as soft and as
familiar as little pets, before
we pull a paw into the light
and shake a truce, instead of fight.

Volume 36, no. 2, 2008

CATHERINE CARTER

Crow Cosmogony

The day we made the world, scattered
shattered sand across the deep
steeps and hollows of the sea,
we were playing with chance,
a stance few other gods admired.
We retired then from creation and let things
sing as they would, go
to whatever end luck called good.
We could, and did, breathe in a platypus here,
a shearwater there – evolution
our solution to dogma and fate,
the weight of always being in charge
of stars, shoals, plague, all that –
but by and large, we let go, let
sweat and thought fall away,
stray like questing possums
or blossoms of blown snow.
So it was. We didn't worry how
our sowing would grow. We went back
to hacking with our thick
black bills at death and waste, harrying
carrion, even as the dead
bled ever more numerous over the new
true-straight stone roads, here
where we shaped the bright turns
and returns of the world, invited
night in: but do that, and you get
what you get. Despised
as flies, we pick through pale grass
for carcasses gone flat and dry;
we rise under your very wheels
from meals scant and cold, bring
strings of gut back to our young. But so
goes the world, when you let it go,
throw yourself in its rolling motion, chance
chance: we live on broken squirrels
in the world we made this way.

Volume 46, no. 1, 2017

MARSHA TRUMAN COOPER

Nesting Boxes

"The feeling heart does not tire of carrying ballast."

—Jane Hirshfield

She knows where
it's legal to bury
the ashes of a human being.
Deep in woods,
she hides her old husband
under land for which
he fought a fire
and won. Wilderness
has attempted a comeback
here, pine again,
almost waist high.
She builds nesting boxes –
the special kind for bluebirds –
and hangs them in the sun
to lose the smell of nails.
In time, she sets them
among the high spruce
that surrounds
saplings in the process
of reclaiming burned space
and his unmarked grave.
The birds arrive.
Every year, a shy
blue circle raises
its generation of song.
She keeps track of the woodpecker –
trouble in a red hat –
lured to the area by
a subdivision's fresh supply
of shingled roofs.
Sure enough,
woodpecker populations
increase,
while gradually
a bluebird region of sky

begins giving up its music.
She baits traps
with suet and chauffeurs
sounds of hammering
to faraway trees
infested with a famous beetle.
She guards her nesting boxes
and the melodies native
to my uncle's place.
She shakes her white head,
asking what we're all coming to –
though she knows –
and turns with her world
which goes around
the other way.

Volume 41, no. 1, 2012

JEFF HARDIN

Woodsmoke

    While driving through the countryside in winter,
    down roads where land is farms, not neighborhoods,
    I'll catch a whiff of woodsmoke hanging faint
    along a fencerow,

                        scan the field to see
    A chimney in the distance spilling out
    slow-motion ghosts to haunt the porch and trees,

    remember the ash that used to tint
    my shoes and coat the stand of figurines
    above the mantel.

                      That simmering hiss
    and a pop of hickory slabs that fell through grates
    into a pan it was my job to dump.
    That silent walk in pitch black February,
    the path I couldn't see

                      but trusted toward,
    no trace of me but breath I sensed inside.

Volume 39, no. 2, 2011

R.T. SMITH

Raptor

In lunar sheen
that is less a pearl
moon than the owl's
skull on the sill,
I consider my own
hungers, the mind
curved like a beak,
every notion torn
like a cornered
siskin or rabbit.
Instead of thought,
I want the soft
touch of owl down,
eyesilver so keen
no strong jaw or
talon is needed, wings
more quiet than
moonlight and a song
so sweet whatever
trembles in tall
grass will accept
its fate with no
howling. As wind
stirs hyssop and
yarrow, I want
surrender, no more
gnawing, a spell
to render me hollow.
I have been
too long ruminant,
too long nocturnal
and alone.

Volume 18, no. 2, 1990

TIM APPLEGATE

The Owl

The river and its aisle of oaks, each new leaf
tipped with the fires of the sun.
The canoe's silent traveler. And at moonrise

a thin stream of smoke
in pencil-sketch branches
as a fish in the distance leaps toward the idea of joy.

Look – in the long
channel of sky above the shallows
an owl is unfolding her body, wing

by beautiful wing: a simple moment
which now, in memory, seems
like the text of a prayer.

The tin cup. The moon's white ashes.
And once again over coffee

ambition, wearing its muddy boots.
   I could have, I should have…
Your hands on my shoulders like rain.

Volume 27, no. 1, 1998

REBECCA BAGGETT

Opossums

Possum after possum strewn along
the mountain road, their guts strung out
like red flags signaling danger, danger
to their unlettered kin. So many I lost count
or no longer noticed, as if I walked past
petals scattered from wind-battered camellias.

But today at the children's zoo, I watched
a possum poke her white face from her nest,
its doorway wrapped for freezing nights
in bright blue and pink fleece, the colors
in which we swaddle our young, watched her tug
the blue one draped over her head to wind it
over her face, then tuck herself back into her nest
for her long day's sleep. Outside the wire,
I stood and mourned at last all her lost kin,

their sharp canny faces,
keen eyes dazzled by the terrible light.

Volume 45, no. 2, 2017

THOMAS PIRKLE

In the Kitchen

>Not starting a fire
>because it's April
>& the dandelions are up yet
>the room as cold as February–
>no sound but stiff fingers
>scratching across a page,
>writing two poems–
>one sour & permanent,
>the other a mad lament
>for the snow
>on the other side of the mountain.

Volume 7, no. 1, 1979

LESLEY WHEELER

Asexual Reproduction

You bastard, I saw you get out of her car.
Every night at one or two, a new episode
broadcast from the street. The window open,
swollen in its jamb. The children closed,
sweating in swirled sheets. An inspector
found black mold on the coils of the old
air conditioner, so until the duct guys
install salvation, everyone lives in the world.

Screaming softens into sobbing. The bastard
says *Nothing happened* and can't even convince
himself. Tree frogs purr in the broken maple.
Someone else's cat chants at our door. My
husband is away again, moving his sick mother.
My kind of sick, the cough, the rashes,
is no cause for worry. Get some good air
and that heart will begin to behave again.

The neighbor's alone now, smoking, phoning
everyone she knows: *I'm gonna call her, text her,
make her life a fucking hell like she did to me.*
By Wednesday it'll just be him and the kid
who's also outside shrieking at the frogs.
I want mommy. But *Baby, you're with daddy now.*
I scratch at poison ivy hives that smolder
in the dark, shapeless as bad feeling.
Don't want to know about anyone's

wrecked life or the lump at midnight o'clock
in my right breast. Sleep's instrumental music,
please, or even the inhuman voice
of a horn or rising breeze. The husband home,
the pulse in a groove. As if a vine would
grow that way, spore land only where they're told.
*Why did you bring me here, I know you're sneaking
around,* she yells, and the syllables waft away,
thriving in the heat, adapted for dispersal.

Volume 43, no. 1, 2014

R.T. SMITH

Watauga Augury

The goldfinch I call
"Parrot" because he out-yellows
any canary, jonquil or
exotic of the jungle,
is pecking millet
like a metronome,
oblivious, it seems,
to the scurry and bicker
aswirl around him,
a matter of territory,
"pecking order," we say,
and the season of need.
Then the jay I named Snitch
because he warns any bird –
thirsty or splashing the bath –
of slinking cat (ginger,
a neighbor's) and will
squawk out, though as usual
it's Parrot who, counter
to my Audubon guide,
really has the grit and spirit
to rush and assail
the would-be intruder, while
a flickery male cardinal
in the privet thicket seeks
to smother his flame
and leave strife to others,
but before long the melee
reverts to peaceful feeding
and a birdsong morning
after this scrap and palaver
over a scatter
of simple seeds,
if in fact the heart is simple
and only a seed.

ANNIE WOODFORD

In the City Woods

That breathe
           Between school and asphalt lake,
Virginia Creeper leaves fall first,
Red negatives with saw-teeth edges

Pasted,
Mid-pulse,
Against dull dirt.

Roots rubbed smooth by bike tires cross the trail.
Each leaf has been seen.
These trees store a record
Of the same floods as us in their rings.

And yet,
A warp and weft —
           Spider web, owl pellet,
The scatter of shadows on box turtle's back —
                    Occasionally gleams
Through the density
Of dying green.

Days are still long.
Half-grown fawns startle here.
Grey foxes bide their invisible time,
Sharp eyes dark stars.

Volume 43, no. 2, 2015

KEVIN KECK

Anniversary of Your Father's Death

You pluck the hair from your left nipple
in the bathroom–I watch you from bed
running your finger over the flesh
where the follicle was uprooted.
This has not been a good day, and here
this single hair with its pinprick removal
is just one more thing.

My parents' house is next to a cemetery,
and when I lived with them I remember how each week
it seemed there was a new stone being birthed from the
      earth,
and how for months people were drawn there,
as though the markers were great anchors
that weighed the whole town, as sandbags hold a hot-air
      balloon
to the ground, so it seemed that had the dead
not been planted there the buildings and streets
would slowly rise and disappear.

This morning I was lying awake
listening to your breath against the gentle hum of the
      refrigerator
in the next room when you shuddered awake. You
had dreamed you were flying, Home,

you had said. But your body was a great weight,
so you were continually pulled again
and again to strange streets, the tops of houses,
unfamiliar woods–whatever you happened to be flying over
At the time, the earth nothing more than a midwife
whose face lingers as a searing whiteness
long after you have been dragged from the dark.

Waking, you worked your fingers into my shirt,
twisting it into knots, and spoke matter of factly about
      your father,
how he turns the earth now, quietly and cleanly,

finally free of the dirt baked into his hands
after years of turning the earth with his fists.

Easing each other back into sleep, I dreamed
of a small town rising from your body: a house,
a little church, stores and streets lined with dogwoods.
And up on a hill, a little graveyard where your father is buried,
and pushing up through his earth a single weed
that will not let you forget.

Volume 25, no. 2, 1997

PAUL MULDOON

Redknots

The day our son is due is the very day
the redknots are meant to touch down
on their long haul
from Chile to the Arctic Circle,
where they'll nest on the tundra
within a few feet
of where they were hatched.
Forty or fifty thousand of them
are meant to drop in along Delaware Bay.

They time their arrival on these shores
to coincide with the horseshoe crabs
laying their eggs in the sand.
Smallish birds to begin with,
the redknots have now lost half their weight.
Eating the eggs of the horseshoe crabs
is what gives them the strength to go on,
forty or fifty thousand of them getting up all at once
as if for a rock concert encore.

(from *Moy Sand and Gravel: Poems*, 2002, reprinted with permission of Farrar, Straus and Giroux)

Volume 31, no. 2, 2003

ROSE MCLARNEY

You Must Know Things By Their Moving Away

From leavings, you may learn the animals. Look for tracks
of bobcats in mud and dust. Droppings and, in them, details

of what fruit (the pits) or meat (the fur) was the fox's feast.
Flattened places in front of the berry bushes where a bear stood,

reaching. Burrow into which a beaver bowed. Path into brush
deer filed along, too slender for your feet to follow.

From far off, you recognize ways your family moves –
their walks, their talking gestures, even with backs turned.

Likewise with birds, you can see whether they are calm or fidgeting
on the branch without ever coming close enough to view markings,

then how the wings look in flight. You must know
things by their moving away. The hand motions

of your husband will stay (as long as he does lift them) the same,
after his first, young face has been furrowed and replaced.

Concentrate on the silhouette slipping into shadow,
all that can be glimpsed from your distance. Be glad

of the field guide, so-named because it was the first book
among the bulky volumes of science with this intent:

Here is a small thing you may carry with you.

Volume 45, no. 2, 2017

GUSTAVO PÉREZ FIRMAT

Old Octopus

In the beginning he had many arms.
Now he bumps along the ocean's floor,
a lone tentacle slowly heaving,
sniffing out the madrepores.

"You say I vent to hide or threaten.
It's not so. Ink is connection.
I vent to embrace. I vent to hold you.
Armless, I yearn, I stay in motion.

My ink is thicker than your water, but
I am so small, a fist without fingers,
and you are everywhere. I do what I do.
I can't swim. I don't sleep. What I do is linger,

wait for the proper current. When it comes
– it is here, now – I flood the deep with longing."

Volume 43, no. 1, 2014

LINDA HOGAN

Black Walnut: Sweet Blood History

From one seed of childhood memories, I recall a stormy night and seeing my grandfather ride his horse toward home through a thunderstorm. I watched through the leaves of a large tree. In each flash of lightning as he came closer, the world was also a bright display of daylight green grass and trees.

Even through the strong odor of rain, from the open window I smelled the powerful soul of the black walnut tree near the window. It had an odor that was unique, a medicinal scent of herb and something fragrant I couldn't name.

I had an affinity for that tree, a love that eventually grew to contain other trees. By day, I liked to put my small fingers in the dark, furrowed bark and let them travel. I considered this particular tree my own in some way, its long leaves that held other leaves and shaped something like a fern, the green cluster of nuts together in young groups until ready to fall. It even had its own unique sound as the warm winds passed through its leaves.

But it was the odor of this tree that really distinguished it from others. It had a beautiful smell I believed. It was strong enough that broken layers of shells or even the leaves kept insects from entering the house.

This one tree grew outside the old, small unpainted home where my grandparents moved after the Great Depression. It was a land of great silences and the dappled light of many trees. I played in the movement of that light, and sometimes I tried to open the two layers of walnut shell, a child seeking mysteries with tools, a hammer or another utensil, but I usually only managed to stain my hands and clothing. That is, until my father stepped in to help. He was gifted enough to impeccably open the shells and remove the meat.

Memory is filled with presences made large, and we were part of a big Chickasaw family with large memories. Our people were strongly those of the land who once cared for grasses, gardens, and trees. We had long been keepers of the Southeastern forests, and nuts were a primary food, so the many nut trees received much attention and care.

In my child's imagination, that particular Oklahoma black walnut tree may have been one of many nut trees growing in the area. It is possible that it permitted other trees to grow in its presence. In all the singular peculiarity of this species, it is a tree with roots stretching far and wide, holding the tree solid while they send out a toxin (juglans) that kills many other trees and brush. A black walnut is choosy about which certain plants and understory are permitted to thrive near or beneath its shadows.

In those young days I didn't know about the ways of plants or their keen intel- ligence. Looking back now, it seems that we were mostly the keepers of stories, not forests. Our lives were created by stories. Many were told at night, without electricity, as we sat outside and listened to the older people talk. Even now, there are times I feel I grew up during the Great Depression, the closing of the banks, and the loss of our lands. I lived through numerous acts of federal corruption and local thefts. I survived living in Indian

Territory before it was the state of Oklahoma and the famous thieves and gangs passed through. There they were safe from the law, and they sought refuge in the caves nearby. Many years later, some of my very young students, two cousins, each individually wrote about their family members saving Bonnie and Clyde from the law, so I wasn't alone in this lived experience of story and our history and its effects on children.

Invariably, as we sat and listened, someone told about the time my grandfather bought a car from his brother. It turned out to be stolen. It was the only car he ever bought. After that he drove only two horses with a wagon to fill the large milk container with water from the community pump. The pump was for the Indians who lived without a source of water. My sister and I rode along and while he filled the milk cans outside, we went inside the general store for a soda or other treat.

But despite that experience of ours, my father told me the story that influenced me greatly. Before land thefts and losses, their own first home had been a large ranch. It was on our family's original allotment land and my grandfather was the kind of man who'd part with no parcel of earth and never a healthy tree. But during the time of war, black walnut was the most valuable wood because it was in great demand for gunstock.

The family went to town one day, and I believe they stopped to visit relatives. Perhaps they stayed to eat. In those days, no one left another home hungry. They might even have spent the night. When they returned, their beautiful black walnut trees had been cut and taken away. It was a terrible loss, and I understood that the loss of the trees mattered not so much financially, but that their disappearance was a loss to the heart, and it was also one more theft from an Indian family who'd lost much already.

All this happened before I was born, when my father was young. But the pain over this loss was never remedied. Even after the last trace of the older generation was gone, the ghosts of the stolen trees have remained with me. They were the trees of my heart, too.

Some time later, the smaller home of my grandmother burned down. By then my grandfather was gone, so my grandmother moved to a small town to be near one of my aunts. Several years later, my father and I were on a journey of memory, collecting oral histories and visiting our family. I wanted to stop at my grandmother's old home, even though it had burned. To our surprise, not far from the black shadow that had been their home, the black walnut tree was still there. It stood older, larger, and shaped a bit differently by the changed currents of air.

After that, I began research on our very long Chickasaw history, including our lives before the explorers and invaders arrived in 1541. Those first violent Europeans wrote about how amazed they were at our forests, how we cared for them, groomed them, and lived from their many offerings. Their botanists wrote the most, so the trees and plants were well documented. Nothing similar existed at the time in Europe. Numerous botanists arrived to take samples back to Europe. They had boxes large enough for trees and smaller boxes for medicinal and other important plants. Few of their samples survived in European conditions, even though greenhouses with controlled temperatures were built for them. I imagine the soil was long dead, missing nutrients and micronutrients necessary to feed and nurture trees or plants from any of the continents they visited.

Perhaps some intuition informed me that forests and plants beyond compare had lived in my blood centuries ago. Then I discovered that black walnut trees were even a larger part of our history. In a book called The Global Forest, Diana Beresford-Kroeger wrote about the large city of the Mississippians called Cahokia, people from which I come. While called a city in history and anthropology books, it was primarily more of a gathering place. What's important is that the population of this place considered a city was larger than London or Paris at the same time in history, from 800-1200 C.E.

Southeastern tribal peoples were mound builders and earth-workers. Our ancestors built numerous effigy mounds, some in the shape of animals and other mysteries, some to accommodate the sky, the sun and moon and constellations. Numbers of these are still in existence, even if little known to many people. Most popular now is the "city" named Cahokia, which is a region of many mounds. A pyramid there is larger than any found in Egypt or the Yucatan. Of over a hundred mounds, one that's most frequently visited is named "Monk's Mound" because French Trappist monks lived there for a time.

For me, the most fascinating fact about this pyramid is that it was completely encircled by black walnut trees. The people who lived there knew these intelligent trees were able to repel certain animals, insects, and parasites. At the same time, the trees attracted others that were beneficial. With their strong scent, they were a valuable presence and may have permitted medicine plants, berries, and other foods to grow beneath them. Their magnificent underground roots spread out a long distance to hold the moist bottomland soil intact. These trees preferred earth near waterways like those where great rivers meet, land given to flooding and easily washed away. This green bottomland is the perfect home for black walnut trees. They held it strong, even during seismic activity, such as the Great Madrid earthquake of 1812 that reversed the direction of the Mississippi River.

The odor I loved of the black walnut tree is the language, maybe even the labor, of this tree. Each tree has its own intelligence. This one dwells among the higher minds.

Its intelligence isn't only the root system, or how many parts of a tree might work together to keep it alive in a complex ecosystem. It draws to it the monarch butterflies that make their migration through this location to feed from this favored tree, the black walnut. So do over two hundred other species of butterfly and moths, including the rare Luna moth. The deer are attracted to its shade, and in these shadows, healing plants like swamp weed, milkweed and wild ginger grow.

Some of these mounds are mysteries. Classes were attended here, and so were performances of drama and music. Some areas were only for worship of our sky and our ancestral beings. Some mounds held the ancestors. One body was found with a tablet in her hand. On one side was a butterfly and on the other were a panther and snake. Constellations and something that appeared to be writing were also there. These were only part of the collected life known by the people, but nothing was known as well as the trees. The black walnut trees were groomed of insects by numerous but now extinct heath hens and passenger pigeons. Other birds protected the trees from those who might break into the sweet liquid inside the bark, once used as a sweetener or syrup for the people.

Because of this tree, the region remained free of unwanted insects, attracted food, and kept the unwanted wildlife at bay, while bringing close the animals that were desirable. The root system, in a riverine bottomland, kept the land intact, and held the world of mounds in place during seismic activity.

Perhaps it is history, but I believe it is truth, that trees are part of the sacred life. The fluid that passes through all things that have lived on our small and amazing planet continues to pass into other lives. It is a world that may be too great for us to take in with only a simple human mind.

Unknown to me, the first tree I remember was a long part of our history through time.

I still think of the black walnut tree I knew as a girl and wonder how many may once have existed in the rich forests of Oklahoma, earlier called Indian Territory, in the time before great deforestation. What I believed was a beautiful, intriguing scent was actually a toxic smell that said, 'Keep away,' to many other trees, to animals, and to insects that might otherwise have harmed it.

Trees are still my sacred world. They are beautiful people. I try to remember to acknowledge them, especially the grandmother and grandfather pine that have grown tall here where I live, old growth trees that have shaped themselves and rooted so perfectly that they've withstood great snows over the years, with branches perfectly spaced to allow air currents to move around them, healthy enough to withstand infestations, and to have remained standing even after the great flood of 2013 created devastation all around them.

As a child, I never knew about nitrogen-fixing plants or trees, or potassium, or the table of elements that is part of our world. I only knew the sound of the wind passing through leaves and carrying the breath of all of the life around us. As it turned out, there were stories older than the ones I heard sitting outside at night, listening to the family speak about older times.

Now I know that all trees are sacred. They are not speechless. It's just that you have to listen with your heart, and at night you may see the stars through branches and know it is all one cosmos, the sky, the ground beneath, and the way sweet fluid moves through our lives.

Volume 45, no. 1, 2016

R.T. SMITH

Gooseneck Loosestrife

Why the loosestrife
won't make it through winter
the botanist would know
and the gardener sleeved
in dirt, the hobbyist in love
with sap and passage,
the way spikes help
hold the sun's ichor
and roots reach
down as tendrils,
fingers. Somehow
beyond my understanding
leaves and petals forming
tiny starbells tell
stem and pistil
or even the sweetest
days of mild wind
and generous light
that night ice is
coming soon to
sheath and strangle
any fiber in reach.
Life will go skeletal
and be trampled.
And yes, today's
rising stems know
to cluster with others
so that the family,
colony, clan, whatever,
can bunch to share
sustenance, almost
a flock of sheep,
which earns this
flower a second name –
Shepherd's Crook –
silent, a question
mark at peace,
the spires unlikely

rife with mites
or tiny beetles,
and without such
pests, loosestrife bows
so courtly in wind
and conducts quiet life
as if blessed and
thereby are seldom
called weeds by even
laymen like me.
Of Asian origin,
the deciduous ornamental
is indicted as
invasive, simply too much
life for the chosen
space, and dies under
the touch of the keen
blade or deadly
chemicals. Its name
in archaic Greek arose
from conviction
among Thracian royals
that boiled leaves
would pacify a maddened
bull. It's all amazing,
and the more lore
I root out and gather,
collect and ponder,
the more placid,
soothed, serene and
riddle-smitten
I myself become.
Oh, I know the solution's
in the root secrets, cells,
nutrients, rainwater's
ruse, the protector's touch.
Yet still, thankfully,
I do not begin to grasp
in my wondering
wandering how these
modest, durable,
deciduous and gentle

wild flowers flower
and perish above ground,
yet in darkness
of heart and season
strifelessly breed.
It is more miracle
than I can sanely sing.

CONTRIBUTORS

Tim Applegate

Tim's poetry and short fiction have appeared in *The Florida Review*, *The South Dakota Review*, and *Lake Effect*, among many other journals and anthologies. He is the author of the poetry collections *At the End of Day* and *Blueprints*, the chapbook *Drydock (and other poems)*, and the crime novels *Fever Tree* and *Flamingo Lane*. Tim recently relocated to southern Indiana where he is working on his next novel and a new chapbook of poems. You can find Tim online at www.timapplegate.net.

Cynthia Atkins

Cynthia Atkins (she/her), originally from Chicago, IL is the author of *Psyche's Weathers*, *In the Event of Full Disclosure*, and *Still-Life With God* (Saint Julian Press 2020), and *Duets*, a collaborative chapbook from Harbor Editions. Her work has appeared in many journals, including *Alaska Quarterly Review*, *BOMB*, *Cider Press Review*, *Diode*, *Cimarron Review*, *Gargoyle*, *Indianapolis Review*, *Lily Poetry Review*, *Los Angeles Review*, *Rust + Moth*, *North American Review*, *Permafrost*, *Plume*, *Tinderbox*, and *Verse Daily*. She earned her MFA from Columbia University and teaches at Blue Ridge Community College. Atkins has earned fellowships and prizes from Bread Loaf Writers' Conference, SWWIM Residency, Virginia Center for the Creative Arts, The Writer's Voice, and Writers@Work. Atkins lives on the Maury River of Rockbridge County, VA. More work and info at: www.cynthiaatkins.com

Sally Atkins

Sally Atkins, Ed.D., REAT, REACE, is a teacher, poet, psychotherapist, researcher, and ritualist. Professor Emerita and founding coordinator of the graduate expressive arts program at Appalachian State University and Core Faculty of the European Graduate School for 20 years, she teaches and consults internationally. Her publications include textbooks, research articles and poetry celebrating the creative process in nature, art and life.

Rebecca Baggett

Rebecca Baggett is the author of the prize-winning collection, *The Woman Who Lives Without Money* (Regal House Publishing, 2022) and four chapbooks, including *God Puts on the Body of a Deer* (Main Street Rag) and *Thalassa* (Finishing Line Press). Recent work appears or is forthcoming in *Asheville Poetry Review*, *The Georgia Review*, *Poetry Daily*, *Salt*, and *The Sun*. She lives with her husband, Elmer Clark, in Athens, GA, where she stewards Little Free Library #110,420, plants native habitat over her quarter-acre, and rejoices in her four-year-old grandson.

Lory Bedikian

Lory Bedikian's second book *Jagadakeer: Apology to the Body* won the 2023 Prairie Schooner/Raz-Shumaker Book Prize in Poetry, published by the University of Nebraska Press. Her first collection *The Book of Lamenting* won the Philip Levine Prize in Poetry. Several of Bedikian's poems received the First Prize Award in the Pablo Neruda Prize for Poetry as part of the 2022 *Nimrod* Literary Awards. She teaches poetry workshops in Los Angeles and elsewhere.

M. Soledad Caballero

M. Soledad Caballero is a Professor of English and Women's Gender and Sexuality Studies at Allegheny College. She is a Macondo and CantoMundo fellow, winner of *Cutthroat: A Journal of the Arts'* 2019 Joy Harjo poetry prize and the 2020 SWWIM's SWWIM-For-the-Fun-of-It contest. Her poems have appeared in the *Missouri Review*, the *Iron Horse Literary Review*, *Ninth Letter*, and other venues. Her essays have been published in *The Hopkins Review*, *Cagibi*, and elsewhere. *I Was a Bell* (2021) won Red Hen Press's 2019 Benjamin Saltman poetry prize, was the 2022 International Association of Autoethnography and Narrative Inquiry book of the year, and was a 2022 International Latino Book Award winner. Her second collection, *Flight Plan*, will be published by Red Hen Press in 2025. She is an avid TV watcher and a terrible birder.

Catherine Carter

Catherine Carter's poetry collections with LSU Press include *Larvae of the Nearest Stars* (2019), *The Swamp Monster at Home* (2012), and *The Memory of Gills* (2006), with *By Stone and Needle* forthcoming in fall 2025. Her work has appeared in Poetry, Ploughshares, RHINO, Tar River Poetry, and Best American Poetry 2009, among others. Born and raised on the eastern shore of Maryland, she now lives in Cullowhee, North Carolina, where she is a professor of English Education at Western Carolina University.

David Childers

David Childers began writing and publishing poetry in the early 1970s, but transitioned into writing and performing songs for a diverse range of audiences, in many different places, in the 1990s. He plays solo and he also plays with a combination of ensembles generally called The Serpents, which can vary from 2 to 5 additional players. He has written and recorded several albums worth of songs, and his songs have been performed by the Avett Bros., and now deceased Scottish singer/songwriter, Jackie Levin. Childers continues to write, record and perform on a regular basis. While past performance venues have ranged from New York to Amsterdam, Mexico, Britain, and several East Coast and West Coast states; in the last few years, he has limited himself to performing mostly in North Carolina. He still writes poetry when the inspiration strikes; and he spends a great deal of his time painting and selling his original art.

Christie Collins

Christie Collins currently teaches writing and literature at Mississippi State University. She has also taught at Louisiana State University in Baton Rouge and Cardiff University in the United Kingdom. Her critical and creative work has been published in *Stirring, Phantom Drift, Kenyon Review Online,* and *North Carolina Literary Review* among others. In 2023, she published her first full-length collection of poems with Eyewear Books/ Black Springs Group in London, titled *The Art of Coming Undone*.

Marsha Truman Cooper

Marsha Truman Cooper was awarded first prize in the New Letters Literary Awards Competition for poetry, received the Bernice Slote Poetry award, and won publication for two poetry chapbooks in blind competitions. "Nesting Boxes" celebrates her great aunt who died in the late 1990s at a ripe old age doing marvelous things right up to the end. She currently studies botanical art full time with two mentors in the UK.

Steven R. Cope

It was 2002 before his first collection of poems, *In Killdeer's Field*, appeared, which included the poem "Ohshon." He has managed some sort of book every couple of years since, most recently from Broadstone Books: *Selected Poems* (2013), *Wa-hita* (2017), and *The Bean Can*, a novel (2018). Winding down a bit now, though *Appalache*, poems, he hopes to have in hand in the spring.

Todd Davis

Todd Davis is the author of eight books of poetry, most recently *Ditch Memory: New & Selected Poems* and *Coffin Honey*, both published by Michigan State University Press. He has won the Midwest Book Award, the Foreword INDIES Book of the Year Bronze and Silver Awards, the Gwendolyn Brooks Poetry Prize, the Chautauqua Editors Prize, and the Bloomsburg University Book Prize. His poems appear in such journals and magazines as *Alaska Quarterly Review, American Poetry Review, Gettysburg Review, Iowa Review, Missouri Review, North American Review, Orion, Southern Humanities Review, Verse Daily,* and *Poetry Daily*. He is an emeritus fellow of the Black Earth Institute and teaches environmental studies and creative writing at Pennsylvania State University's Altoona College.

Hilda Downer

Hilda Downer is the author of four collections of poetry, the most recent, *Wiley's Last Resort*, in 2022. Her second book, *Sky Under the Roof*, was a Nautilus Golden Poetry Winner. She taught English at Appalachian State University as an adjunct while also working as a psychiatric nurse for almost 30 years. Her love of teaching poetry was fulfilled as a volunteer in local elementary schools and currently to senior citizens. She has been published in numerous journals and anthologies such as *Bloodroot* and, most recently, *Crossing the Rift*. She holds an MFA from Vermont College and is a long term member of the Southern Appalachian Writers Cooperative, the Appalachian Studies Association, and the North Carolina Writers Conference. She grew up in Bandana of Mitchell County, NC, and lives outside of Boone. She has two sons, one a professional fiddler and the other a visual artist/photographer.

Gustavo Pérez Firmat

Gustavo Pérez Firmat's imaginative writing has been published in *The Paris Review*, *Ploughshares*, *The Southern Review*, *The Carolina Quarterly*, *Michigan Quarterly Review*, and other journals. His most recent book is *My Favorite Monster* (2024), a volume of translations from the Spanish. He is the David Feinson Professor Emeritus of Humanities at Columbia University. His website: gustavoperezfirmat.com.

Jeff Hardin

Jeff Hardin is the author of seven collections of poetry, most recently *Watermark*, *A Clearing Space in the Middle Of Being*, and *No Other Kind of World*. His work has been honored with the Nicholas Roerich Prize, the Donald Justice Prize, and the X. J. Kennedy Prize.

Patrick Hicks

Patrick Hicks is the author of over ten books, including *Adoptable*, *This London*, *The Commandant of Lubizec*, *In the Shadow of Dora*, and *Across the Lake*. He is the Writer-in-Residence at Augustana University and he also teaches in the MFA program at the University of Nevada Reno at Lake Tahoe.

Linda Hogan

Linda Hogan (Chickasaw) is a poet and author whose first novel, *Mean Spirit* (1990) was a finalist for the Pulitzer Prize. She is Professor Emerita at the University of Colorado and the Writer-in-Residence for the Chickasaw Nation. Her published works of poetry include *Dark, Sweet: New and Selected Poems* (2014) and *Indios* (2012). She has also written nonfiction works, essays, and served as an editor for anthologies on spirituality. She was awarded the Thoreau Prize from PEN in 2016, the Native Arts and Culture Award in 2018, and the LA Review of Books-UC Riverside Department of Creative Writing Lifetime Achievement Award in 2022. She continues to work as a lecturer and reader of her own work.

Kevin Keck

Kevin Keck is a native of North Carolina and a graduate of the Syracuse University MFA program in creative writing. He is the author of the books *Oedipus Wrecked* and *Are You There God? It's Me. Kevin*. He lives in South Carolina where he teaches at College of Charleston.

Basil King

Born in the UK in 1935, immigrated to the USA at age twelve, King began studies at Black Mountain College in 1951. After college studies and time in San Francisco, New York City, and Montana, where he worked under Peter Voulkos, he ultimately settled in New York City's Lower East Side–and then Brooklyn. In 1985, following his first return trip to the UK, he began to write seriously and has since published both chapbooks and full length collections of poetry. His early work painting abstract expressionist works grew into a new approach to art employing fluid forms that combine abstraction, surrealism, and figuration. Now in his 8th decade, he lives in Brooklyn and paints and writes daily.

Sarah Kennedy

Sarah Kennedy is the author of the five-part Tudor historical fiction series, *The Cross and the Crown*, which includes *The Altarpiece, City of Ladies, The King's Sisters, Queen of Blood,* and *Worlds End*. She has also published a stand-alone novel, *Self-Portrait, with Ghost*, as well as seven books of poems. A professor of English at Mary Baldwin University in Staunton, Virginia, Sarah Kennedy holds a PhD in Renaissance Literature and an MFA in Creative Writing. She has received grants from both the National Endowment for the Arts, the National Endowment for the Humanities, and the Virginia Commission for the Arts. Please visit Sarah at her website: http://sarahkennedybooks.com.

Anne Marie Macari

Anne Marie Macari is the author of five books of poetry, most recently *Heaven Beneath* (Persea, 2020) and *Red Deer* (Persea, 2015). Macari's first book, *Ivory Cradle*, won the Honickman/APR First Book Prize in 2000, chosen by Robert Creeley. Her poetry and essays have been widely published in magazines such as *The Iowa Review, Field,* and *APR*.

Ed Madden

Ed Madden is a professor of English at the University of South Carolina, where he teaches Irish literature, creative writing, and queer studies. He is the author of six books of poetry, most recently *A pooka in Arkansas*, winner of the Hillary Tham prize from Word Works.

Linda Malnack

Linda Malnack has published two poetry chapbooks, *21 Boxes* (dancing girl press) and *Bone Beads* (Paper Boat Press). Her poetry appears in *Prairie Schooner, The Madison Review, The Ilanot Review, Cloudbank,* and elsewhere. Linda is a Poetry Editor for *Crab Creek Review*.

Rose McLarney

Rose McLarney's collections of poems are *Colorfast, Forage.* and *Its Day Being Gone* (Penguin Books) and *The Always Broken Plates of Mountains* (Four Way Books). She is co-editor of *A Literary Field Guide to Southern Appalachia* (UGA Press) and *Southern Humanities Review*. Rose is Lanier Endowed Professor of Creative Writing at Auburn University.

Robert Morgan

Robert Morgan is the author of several books of poems, including *Terroir* (2011) and *Dark Energy* (2015). He has published ten books of fiction, among them the New York Times bestseller *Gap Creek*, and, more recently, *Chasing the North Star* (2016), and *In the Snowbird Mountains and Other Stories* (2023). His works of nonfiction include *Lions of the West* (2011), the national bestseller *Boone: A Biography* (2007), and *Fallen Angel: The Life of Edgar Allan Poe* (2023). Recipient of awards from the Guggenheim Foundation and the American Academy of Arts and Letters, he is currently Kappa Alpha Professor of English (Emeritus) at Cornell University.

Paul Muldoon

Paul Muldoon was born in Ireland in 1951 and moved to the United States in the mid 1980s after a successful career working for the BBC. He is the author of fifteen poetry collections, most recently *Joy in Service on Rue Tagore*, as well as smaller poetry collections, children's books, criticisms, and radio and television drama. From 1999 to 2004 he was a Professor of Poetry at Oxford University and has taught at Princeton since 1987. He served as the poetry editor at *The New Yorker* from 2007 to 2017. He has received numerous awards, including the 2004 Shakespeare Prize, the 2017 Queen's Gold Medal for Poetry, the 2018 Seamus Heaney Award for Arts & Letters, and the 2024 Premio di Poesia Sinestetica. He currently resides in New York with his family.

Thomas Pirkle

Thomas Pirkle is a poet and translator who currently lives in a small village in the mountains of southern Spain. He has published in numerous literary journals in both the US and Ireland, where he formerly resided. In 2020 he published *Eyes of Water: Selected Poems of José Angel Valente*.

Benito Del Pliego

Benito del Pliego (Spain, 1970) is a poet, translator, and professor at Appalachian State University. His latest book of poetry is *Integral—dietario reunido*, (Richmond: Ed. Casa Vacía). A bilingual edition of his *Fábula/Fable* appeared in 2016. His poems have been included in numerous anthologies, such as Forrest Gander's *Panic Cure: Poetry from Spain for the 21st Century*, or Joseph Bathanti and David Potorti's *Crossing the Rift: North Carolina Poets on 9/11 & Its Aftermath*.

Rita Sims Quillen

Rita Quillen's most recent poetry book, *Some Notes You Hold* (Madville 2020) has received a Bronze Medal from the Feathered Quill Book Awards, a finalist listing for poetry in the American Writing Awards, and is a Bonus Book for the 2023 International Pulpwood Queens and Timber Guys Book Club. Her novel, *Wayland*, published by Iris Press in 2019, is the March 2022 Bonus Book of the Month for the International Pulpwood Queens and Timber Kings Book Club. It is a sequel to her first novel, *Hiding Ezra* (Little Creek Books, 2014). Her poetry collection, *The Mad Farmer's Wife*, published in 2016 by Texas Review Press, a Texas A&M affiliation, was a finalist for the Weatherford Award in Appalachian Literature from Berea College. One of six semi-finalists for the 2012-14 Poet Laureate of Virginia, she has received three Pushcart nominations, and a Best of the Net nomination in 2012, and was the 2021 honoree of the Emory and Henry College Appalachian Literary Festival. She lives, farms, writes songs, and takes photographs at Early Autumn Farm in southwestern Virginia. Read more at www.ritasimsquillen.com.

Liz Robbins

Liz Robbins' fourth full-length collection, *Night Swimming*, won the 2023 Cold Mountain Press Book Contest. Her other collections are *Freaked*, *Play Button*, and *Hope, As the World Is a Scorpion Fish*. Her chapbooks are *Fire Carousel* and *Girls Turned Like Dials*.

James Silas Rogers

James Silas Rogers is the author of two poetry collections, *Sundogs* (2006) and *The Collector of Shadows* (2019), as well as an essay collection about cemeteries, *Northern Orchards: Places Near the Dead.* (2014). Five of his pieces have been selected as "notables" in the annual *Best American Essays* volumes. He has also published widely on Irish writing.

R.T. Smith

R. T. Smith founded *Cold Mountain Review*, then edited *Southern Humanities Review*. In June of 2018 he retired from Washington and Lee as writer-in-residence and after 23 years of editing Shenandoah. His most recent book is *Doves in Flight* (stories), and a collection of poems, *Summoning Shades*, released in 2019.

Virgil Suárez

Virgil Suárez is a widely published poet, writer, and artist living in Fucked Up, Florida.

G.C. Waldrep

G.C. Waldrep's most recent books are *feast gently* (Tupelo, 2018), winner of the William Carlos Williams Award from the Poetry Society of America; *The Earliest Witnesses* (Tupelo/Carcanet, 2021); and *The Opening Ritual* (Tupelo, 2024). Recent work has appeared in *American Poetry Review, Poetry, Paris Review, Ploughshares, New England Review, Yale Review, The Nation, New American Writing, Conjunctions,* and other journals. Waldrep lives in Lewisburg, Pa., where he teaches at Bucknell University.

Janet Lee Warman

Janet Lee Warman, Professor Emerita of English at Elon University in North Carolina, currently divides her time between Burlington, North Carolina, and Richmond, Virginia. She has had poems published in journals nationally and internationally, including *Rappahannock Review*, *Main Street Rag*, *Slipstream* and *Spillway*. In 2016, she published her chapbook, *Lake Diving*. Her current retirement passions are travel, Court TV, and collecting art.

Lesley Wheeler

Lesley Wheeler, Poetry Editor of *Shenandoah*, is the author of six poetry collections, including *Mycocosmic* (Tupelo Press, March 2025) and *The State She's In*. Her other books include the hybrid memoir *Poetry's Possible Worlds* and the novel *Unbecoming*. Her poems and essays have appeared in *Poets & Writers*, *Pleiades*, *Poetry*, *Ecotone*, and *Massachusetts Review*.

Annie Woodford

Annie Woodford is the author of *Bootleg* (Groundhog Poetry Press, 2019) and *Where You Come from Is Gone* (Mercer UP, 2022), recipient of the 2022 Weatherford Award for Appalachian Poetry. Her micro-chapbook, *When God Was a Child*, was published by Bull City Press in 2023. In 2024, she was awarded the Guy Owen Prize by Southern Poetry Review. Her third poetry collection will be published in 2025 by Pulley Press.

Catherine Young

Catherine Young is author of the ekphrastic memoir *Black Diamonds: A Childhood Colored by Coal* and the ecopoetry collection *Geosmin* (Midwest Book Awards Silver Medal Winner). Her prose and poetry are published in anthologies and literary journals internationally and nationally. She worked as a national park ranger, farmer, educator, and mother. She deeply believes in the use of story for transforming the world. Find her Landward podcasts and writings at: http://www.catherineyoungwriter.com/.